A MAGIC CIRCLE BOOK

THE TWO GIANTS

retold by **EVE BUNTING**
illustrated by **ERIC VON SCHMIDT**

THEODORE CLYMER
SENIOR AUTHOR, READING 360

GINN AND COMPANY
A XEROX COMPANY

M. P. BURKE

Library of Congress Catalog Card Number: 77–153913

International Standard Book Number: 0-663-22989-8

Crossing the Irish Sea between Ireland and Scotland is the Giant's Causeway. It is a long line of tall stone columns which are so close together that the line looks like a road. Some of the columns appear above the surface of the sea and others are completely hidden beneath the sea. Scientists say that the columns were formed long ago by hot liquid rock which bubbled through the earth's crust. Irishmen, however, know better. This, they say, is what really happened.

Finn MacCool, the Irish giant, was the only giant in all of Ireland. He had never seen another and so he thought he was the only giant in all the world. Finn lived with his wife, Oonagh, on the top of a cliff outside the town of Dunmill. The people of the town said, "Finn MacCool is as good a big man as ever wore a hat." Finn often helped them with the potato digging and bringing in the hay, and the people thought he was worth more than ten men put together.

4

One day a sailor came with a message for Finn MacCool. He said that the message was from Culcullen, the Scottish giant. The sailor said that Culcullen was very angry because he had learned about Finn MacCool. Culcullen had always thought that he was the only giant in the world.

"He's daring you to a fight to the death," said the sailor. "And I for one think Culcullen will be the winner. Not that I want him to win, mind you, for he's an old curwheeble and liked by no one. But then, I suppose if every fellow was as good as his neighbor thought he should be, we'd all be saints in heaven!"

The people of the town trembled with fear, for an angry curwheeble of a giant was not good to have around. Finn MacCool trembled too. He was born peaceful and never felt the need to fight.

6

"How big is this Culcullen?" Finn MacCool asked the sailor.

"He's bigger than you," said the sailor. "He's so big that he couldn't wear a top hat to his own wedding for fear it would crack open the sky!"

"Aaragh," said the people of Dunmill, and they squinted at the sky to see how high it was.

"How broad is this Culcullen?" Finn MacCool asked the sailor.

"He's broader than you," said the sailor. "He's so broad that he has to walk sideways towards the sun to keep his shadow from darkening the earth!"

"Aaragh," said the people of Dunmill, and they looked fearfully at the quiet sea.

"How strong is this Culcullen?" Finn MacCool asked the sailor.

"He's stronger than you," said the sailor. "He's so strong that he turns his house upside down and shakes it every week so his lazy wife has no need to sweep the floors."

"Aaragh," said the people of Dunmill, and they huddled together for comfort.

"How will he get here?" Finn MacCool asked. "Surely there's not a boat strong enough to carry a giant from Scotland to Ireland."

"He told me to tell you that he's building a causeway from there to here, and when he gets here, he'll finish you off, take over your land, and make slaves of your people."

"Aaragh," cried the people of Dunmill, and they looked to Finn for protection.

Finn scratched his head. "I'll think on it," he said. "But there's no use in you people looking to me for protection. You might as well look for feathers on a frog's back."

8

By the next morning the news about Culcullen had spread, and the people gathered from miles around to look across the sea to Scotland. Far off in the distance they could see a figure that looked no bigger than a blade of grass.

"It's Culcullen," they whispered, and they looked at one another in horror. "He'll be on top of the Ailsa Craig by night."

Finn MacCool wiped his brow with the tablecloth he used for a handkerchief and reached for Oonagh's hand. "He'll be just about to the Ailsa Craig by night," he told her, "and that's halfway between Ireland and Scotland."

By noon the people could see the spray rising as Culcullen crashed the rocks into the water to build the causeway. That night he sat on top of the big Ailsa Craig and washed his feet in the Irish Sea.

"Finn MacCool," he roared, and his voice was louder than the booming of the waves in the devil's washtub at storm tide. "We'll see tomorrow who is king of the giants — Culcullen or MacCool!" Strange wild fish appeared from the bottom of the sea at the sound of his voice.

10

Finn MacCool scratched his head thoughtfully. "I'm thinking I'm no match for that one," he said at last.

The sailor chuckled. "That you're not," he said. "You're no match for him at all."

"One thing I forgot to ask you," Finn MacCool said. "How smart is Culcullen?"

"Well," said the sailor, "he's as smart as my Aunt Bertha's stupid old cow and a dumber beast never chewed cud."

"So," Finn said, scratching his head again. "He's bigger than me and broader than me and stronger than me and madder than me — but begorrah, if I'm not smarter than your Aunt Bertha's old cow, I'll chew cud myself!" Finn turned to the people standing around him. "All right," he said, "there's work to be done. There'll be no sleep for anyone in Dunmill this night." And he told the people his plan.

12

All through the night by the light of huge lamps, the men of the town chopped down trees and worked with their hammers and nails. The women sewed till the first light of dawn appeared. Then all was ready.

When Culcullen began work again in the morning, he was singing and the sound of his voice set the seagulls to screeching and swooping. The sky was so full of them that it looked like night.

"Aaragh," said the people to one another. "This Culcullen is a terrible creature altogether. Who would have thought that there could be two giants so different as the good MacCool and this one?"

At last, when Culcullen set his great feet on the Irish shore, he gave such a mighty roar that the earth trembled, and every peat stack and hay-stack in all of Ireland tumbled to the ground. "I'm here!" he said. "Lead me to MacCool!"

The people of Dunmill stared in wonder. Culcullen was so tall that he wore the clouds around his shoulders for a cloak. And only the people with the keenest eyes could see up as far as his face.

15

"Good sir," yelled Michael Mor, the town baker. "Finn MacCool wished to be here to meet you, but he was called away to fight the Welsh giant, Dalwyn. MacCool will finish him off before dinnertime, and then he'll be happy to give you as fine a fight as you've ever had. He invites you to go to his house on Raskin Head and share his meal. He'll be there soon."

"That's very nice of him," said Culcullen. "I like to eat before fighting."

Michael Mor led the way to Finn MacCool's house. Oonagh stood in her front yard, rocking a giant cradle. Its rockers were the trunks of two mighty oaks, and ten more oaks curved around its sides.

"My husband has another giant to take care of, sir," said Oonagh, with a smile that hid her fear. "He took our four grown sons with him, but I stayed behind to greet you and care for our baby."

16

"I thought I saw Finn MacCool standing on a cliff as I crossed the Irish Sea," said Culcullen, frowning.

"No indeed, sir, that was this child. He is small for his age, but he's walking early. I fear he takes after my side of the family and will never be as big as his father or his brothers."

Culcullen peered into the cradle. There, dressed in a baby dress and bonnet, lay Finn MacCool. He was pulling the links from a chain with his teeth, which was the only act of strength he had ever learned. Oonagh slapped his hands and took the chain from him.

"I declare," she said angrily. "Somebody has given this to you to play with again. You'll crack your first teeth, you will!"

17

Culcullen's eyes opened wide. "You say this is your youngest?" he asked.

"Aye," said Oonagh, "and I'm fair ashamed to say that he's mine. But then, the poor wee thing can't help it. They say there's a runt in every litter. But one thing I'll say for him — he's got as bad a temper as his father and brothers!"

Culcullen cleared his throat, and in doing so, blew the roof off Oonagh's house.

"Oh, don't worry, it doesn't matter," Oonagh said with a smile. "We'll soon have it right again. Last week this wee baby sneezed and blew the whole house down the hill."

Culcullen's face grew pale. "Jakers," he thought to himself. "If this is the size of the baby, what size must the bad-tempered father be? And nobody told me about the four grown sons!"

19

"Woman," Culcullen said, "I have an early meeting to attend in Scotland, and I have no time to sit around here. Tell Finn MacCool I'm sorry I missed him. I'll be glad to fight him any time in Scotland if he would come to my side of the Irish Sea."

"Ah, yes," said Oonagh. "And now that you've built the causeway, it will be very easy for him to cross over. He'll likely come after you — he and the boys — tomorrow or Sunday the latest."

20

"Good, good!" Culcullen roared, hurrying down the hillside.

"Good-by, good-by!" the people of Dunmill called to Culcullen as he started across the causeway on his way home. They waved their handkerchiefs in the air and called, "Come back soon," for they had been taught that that was the polite thing to say to a parting guest. But they didn't think Culcullen would understand because they shouted it in Gaelic.

Anyway, they didn't see how Culcullen could hear them with all the noise he made, ripping up the stones of the causeway as he went along, and flinging them all into the sea.   Sure he could build another road, but since he was rushing away, it didn't look as if he'd be in any hurry to come back!

22

ABCDEFGHIJK   7654321
PRINTED IN THE UNITED STATES OF AMERICA